To Bill.

May each and every precious day bring you great happiness, inspiring discoveries and exciting challenges. And may all your aspirations be fulfilled. Good luck!

Richard Cripwell.

RICHARD CRIPWELL

The Boogle Stump

ATLAS BOOKS
OXFORD

Published in Great Britain in 1995 by
Atlas Books Ltd., 1 - 5 Broad Street, Oxford, OX1 3AW, UK

Printed and bound in Great Britain

Cover design by Nicky Ellis
Illustrations by Kathryn Lamb

British Library Cataloguing in Publication Data

A catalogue record for this book is available
from the British Library

ISBN 1 900236 00 1

To Margery Humfrey, my adored and wonderful Grandmother, who, through pure love, faith and infinite wisdom, has not only shown me how to fully appreciate the true beauty of the world and the miracle of life, but has also instilled in me exquisite happiness by teaching me how always to seek the good rather than the evil in everyone and everything.

R.C.

The Land of Evol Dictionary
(Evol to English)

Bamble Boots	:	boots which are made from the outer skin of a boogle top, once chewed and spat out by Snapperclogs.
Boogle	:	a sort of mushroom.
Clob	:	a troll-like little person of Evol.
Grazzle	:	grass which has gone to seed.
Jioota	:	a tall tree of the woodland.
Noblets	:	nuts, berries and other fruits which have fallen to the ground.
Stiggle	:	an ant-like little creature of Evol.
Tubbly	:	rounded in shape and of cuddly appearance.
Trumble	:	for Clobs it means to trot and tumble in one action. For other creatures it simply means to go about.
Tuggle	:	vine.
Weasily	:	very, very carefully.

Notes

Archio is pronounced 'arkyo'

Jioota is pronounced 'yewta'

Mao is pronounced 'mow' (like cow)

WELCOME

to

the

land

of

EVOL

Evil ?

No!

Evol . . .

and these two words must
never be confused . . . because
in the land of Evol there is no
Evil.

Turn the letters of Evol
around, and it spells . . .

Love

— ♦ —

so, in other words . . .

it

is

the

Land of Love

Let me introduce

you to some of the

inhabitants of

Evol

Meet

Glibalobs

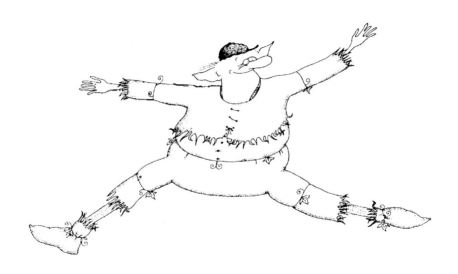

Glibalobs is a born teacher.　　He is
always the one with the ideas . . .

though often not very good
ones.

He is a lot taller than his
friend Fu, long limbed and
gangly.   He always has to be
on the move (except when
sitting on a boogle stump, of
course).   He is not a fidget,
just very active.   And that
doesn't necessarily mean that
he gets anywhere faster or
more efficiently than anyone
else.   He goes around in
circles a lot, jumps up and
down and enjoys star-jumping
(in his clob-like way).

He has a friendly face, and
you can't help liking him.

and now, let us say hello to

Fu

Fu is short and tubbly and always puffed out (exhausted, I mean). He trumbles with a limp - no deformity, he just trumbles like that.   He is always left behind and he is always the odd one

out.   You cannot help but
feel sorry for Fu.   'It's a hard
life' - but he would never give
up.   He is always taking on
jobs which are quite beyond
him, but he goes to all lengths
to complete the task he has
undertaken.

Fu loves the snow.   And
when it does snow, he packs it
all over his face to cool himself
down, so much so that often
you can't actually see his face
underneath it all.

Fu is totally adorable.   He is
kind and thoughtful, and
always the first to help.

But there is something rather
wistful about Fu.

and here is

Gramblesnip

Gramblesnip is very quiet, rather
nervous, and always reserved.
He has a cool temper, observes a
great deal but speaks very
infrequently.   He notices

everything and his mind is
always busy forming opinions
and conclusions (but he keeps
them to himself).   He is a
true thinker.   He would not
say anything unless he was
absolutely right.   He watches
other clobs doing silly things,
and then does it himself the
right way.   But he doesn't
need attention or praise - he
just does it.   He has a kind
face, again he is likeable,
although it would be nice to
know what was going on in
his mind.   He is always
sensible and never mischievous.
He eats good food always.
He would never settle for old
bracken if he could travel
further and find new bracken.

And let us meet

Snapperclogs

Snapperclogs is the
Good Green Dragon.
His fire ran out a long time
ago, and his claws are blunt.
Sometimes he tries to look fierce, but
fails dismally.   His belly sags, and
often, especially when he has just
eaten, it drags along the ground.   So
he has to find a couple of friends to
tie a vine around his middle so that
he can walk.   If there are no friends
around, he simply has to wait until

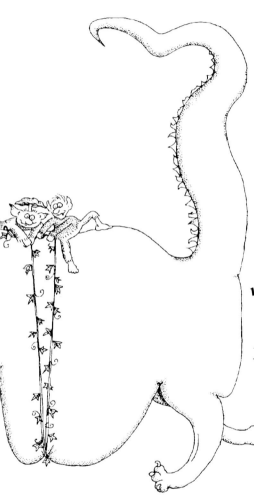

someone passes. Often, as a favour in return, he will 'give a lift' to whoever ties the vine around his middle. Snapperclogs adores youngsters. He has no family. He doesn't know where he came from. One wonders what will happen when Snapperclogs dies. He is very much a Grandfather figure. He is totally harmless and kind and, like Fu, a little wistful.

and now I must tell you about

Fig

Fig is God of Evol.   Fig is very
colourful, although it is difficult

to determine his shape.   But
he does have a face, a very
warm face, and warm,
comforting hands.   And one
can tell when his mood
changes (which it often does).

Fig can see everyone and
everything all the time.
Although he is God, and all
loving, he is frighteningly
powerless, and, in times of
trouble, there is very little that
he can physically do.

We will meet more inhabitants of
The Land of Evol in a moment or
two.

But first of all, let me tell you
about the boogle . . .

A boogle is a sort of mushroom . . .

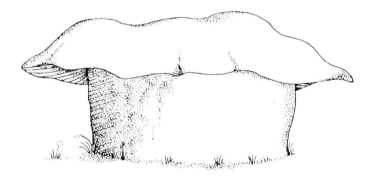

but it is no ordinary sort of mushroom. As fast as boogles grow, their heads are eaten off by Snapperclogs . . .

So only the stump remains.

For Snapperclogs its just food.
But little does he know that
he is indeed doing everyone
else a lot of good too.

For when the head of a boogle
is eaten off, the stump turns
to stone . . .

like a fossil.

But it is a very special kind of stone.

It is alive,

very sensitive,

and

very wise.

And it sends patters of

love into the Earth

where Fig

cannot reach.

. . . yet only when it is perched
upon weasily.

But the boogle stump

is always asleep

. . . and if
the boogle stump is
woken up, it turns back
into a headless mushroom,
withers,
and dies.

And now, I shall tell you

The

Story

Glibalobs and Fu

hill

the

up

trumbled

and perched weasily

on

a

boogle stump

They chortled together
about life, and about
how much they love
being alive, and about
the many things they
want to do - but how
there never seems to
be enough time to do
them all.

"I wish I could go to
sleep more easily at
darkness . . ."
said Fu,

" . . . but I cannot,
because I'm always too
excited about the next
day."

Glibalobs replied

"You should dream like
me, Fu.   It's just as
much fun as all the
many things we do in
the daylight - only you
can sleep at the same
time!"

Fu said

"I've never been able to
  dream.   How do you
  do it Glibalobs?"

and Glibalobs answered
  authoritatively

"You have to think about
  all the best things
  in the Land and then
  Fig decides which one
  you dream about."

6

Fu continued wistfully

"All I can ever think
about before going to
sleep is taking off my
bamble boots - but I
usually go to sleep
before getting around
to it.
Do you think that is
why I don't dream,
Glibalobs?"

"You must think about boogles and Snapperclogs, the Old Oak Tree, and all the fun we have, and all the trumbling we do - and you must always say thank you to Fig."

Fu looked puzzled.

"Why thank you?"

Glibalobs enlightened Fu.

"Because Fig looks after us, and gives us everything we have."

Scratching his head, Fu
thought for half a
second and declared

"Snapperclogs gave me my
boots."

Glibalobs replied
"But Fig gave Snapperclogs
the knowledge to make
them and the materials
to make them with."

"How do you know?"
asked Fu inquisitively.

"Because Fig told me,"
Glibalobs explained. "Fig
tells me lots of things.
He tells me things every
time I sit on a Boogle
Stump."

Fu put his head in his hands and muttered "I don't think Fig likes me."

"Of course Fig likes you" Glibalobs exclaimed. "Fig likes everyone. You must talk to him, and listen, and wait."

They looked into each other's eyes and then Fu looked up to the sky.

"Fig ? Can you hear me?"

There was silence and no reply from Fig.

"See, I told you he doesn't like me" babbled Fu disappointedly.

Glibalobs persisted. "You must be patient, you must work hard and concentrate. It's not easy."

After another brief pause, Fu continued.

"Fig?"

There was silence for a longer period.

Then Fig's voice filled the land around them as he proclaimed

"OF COURSE I CAN HEAR YOU, FU."

11

Elated, Fu leapt from the
    boogle stump and
    shouted out gleefully

"He spoke to me,
    he spoke to me!
    He heard me,
        he heard me!

Do you think he can **see**
    me?"

"OF COURSE I CAN
    SEE YOU, FU."
        Fig answered.

"You see," professed
    Glibalobs,
    "you must have faith
        in him, you must
            believe in him."

"Oh I'm so happy,
  I'm so happy!
I'm going to go and tell
  everyone that Fig spoke
  to me."

Fu trumbled off speedily,
  jumping up and down
  and singing to himself
  gladly.

Fu's Song

Ha ha hee   Ho ho hoo   Ha ha hee   Ha ha hoo   Ha ha hee   Ho ha ho

Ha ha hee   Ha ha hoo   Fig spoke to me,   he saw me too!   All I needed was a   little clue.   He

answered my call, its   true,   its true, its   true !   Ha ha hee   Ho hoo hoo

14

Ha ha hee   Ha ha hoo   Ha ha hee   Ho ho hoo, He   Spoke to me, he saw me too!

Ha ha hee   Ho ho hoo   He he hoo   Ha ha hoo

15

Meanwhile, Gramblesnip was minding his own business in the undergrowth by the spring of the Silver River, weaving pampas to make a basket for collecting forest nuts. But, as always, he was listening intently to his friends' conversation.

He trumbled up to the boogle stump and perched beside Glibalobs. He said nothing but looked into the sky and closed his eyes.

Glibalobs turned himself around and looked at Gramblesnip.

There was a pause and Glibalobs said

"Hallo Gramblesnip"

"Hallo Glibalobs" replied Gramblesnip.

And they began to chortle.

Afar down in the valley
of the Silver River,
Snapperclogs, the good
green dragon was
slapping his long,
bespottled tongue around
his hot and flobberly
lips having just finished
a delectable feast of
boogle tops, when his better
ear hearkened at the
melodies of Fu trumbling
down the hill towards him.

"Hallo, Snapperclogs!"
    hailed Fu excitedly.

"Hallo, Fu,"
    grunted Snapperclogs.

And Fu told
    Snapperclogs of his
    experience.

By the time Fu had finished chortling, Snapperclogs' belly was so full of boogle tops that it had sagged all the way down to the ground.

"Just a moment," said
Fu, "I'll go and find
you a long, strong
tuggle."

Fu trumbled off into the
scrub of the woodland,
chattering all the
while and leaving
Snapperclogs quite
unable to move. He
soon found an old,
tall jioota tree with a
fine, green tuggle just
long enough to reach
all the way around a
fine green dragon full
of boogle tops.

21

Fu clambered up the tuggle, and, swinging fervently to and fro, he pulled and twisted until it was wrenched from the old jíoota's branches. There was a crack, a rustle and a crash, then a wallop, a thud and a squawk as what seemed like half the tree tumbled down upon Fu burying him from toes to nose.

But it wasn't part of
the tree at all, it was
the house of Archio,
the Great Bird of the
Valley.

Fu nervously peered through the top of the heap of scrub, leaves and grazzle, and gulped with surprise as Archio flipped and fluttered her way out of her demolished home.

"Oh no, what have I done?" asked Fu innocently. "I'm sorry Archio, I didn't know you were nesting here today!"

"Don't worry, Fu," squawked Archio, "I'm used to it!"   (For Archio never has much luck with her nests - they always topple down in one way or another).

"Quickly, Archio, I must help you build another nest," said Fu.

"I won't be a moment Snapperclogs!" he hollered across the woodland to his patiently waiting friend.

"But we don't have any grazzle," chirped Archio.

"Don't worry," assured Fu, "just leave it to me."

Without delay Fu set about building a magnificent new home for Archio in the old jíoota tree, but soon he became hopelessly tangled up in the branches, bracken and twigs and, before long, he had become very much a part of the nest himself.

"I told you we needed grazzle" Archio yarked as she dismantled the nest again to unravel Fu.

"Come on, Fu!" she cried. "Let us go and find Snapperclogs. I will help you with the tuggle and then you can come with me to the Stiggle Village to collect some grazzle from Lump."

"Oooo yes, yes," agreed Fu with bundles of enthusiasm, "then we can see Gossip, Mao and Beetle too!"

So Archio held one end of the tuggle in her beak, flitting frantically above the tree tops, whilst Fu trumbled through the scrub, weaving in and out of the tuggles and jioota trees, over and under the branches, stumps and boulders.

Snapperclogs gave a huge bellow of relief when he sighted them at last coming out of the woodland.

"I'm sorry, Snapperclogs," said Fu.
"We had a little mishap."

After a long struggle
with much squawking,
heaving and groaning,
Fu and Archio
succeeded in tying the
long, green tuggle
around Snapperclogs'
belly, allowing him to
travel onwards.

"Now, where would you both like to go?" asked Snapperclogs, eager to return the favour.

"Oh thank you Snapperclogs," cheered Fu. "Could you take us to the Stiggle Village to see Gossip, Mao and Beetle?"

"Yeeaawk!" Archio cried. "And Lump too, so we can collect some grazzle for my nest!"

"An excellent idea," trumped Snapperclogs.

"I haven't been to the Stiggle Village for a very long time - and I wouldn't mind dropping by at the Great Hillock of Blue Boogles!"

"Hold on tightly" he advised.

And Snapperclogs clomped along, through the lush, green valley, across the Silver River and over the old stone walls, his teeth clattering all the while and his tail swooping around in circles.

Suddenly Snapperclogs
flopped.
"I am over puffed"
he steamed
exhaustedly.
"Do you mind if I take
a rest?" he asked
politely.

Snapperclogs stretched
out, his head propped
up by his forefeet,
with one eye open,
dosing but not allowed
to sleep for the games
of Fu and Archio - his
ears, wings and feet
being used as swings
and hiding places.

"Oh I don't know what we would do without you Snapperclogs" said Fu appreciatively. "Please don't go to sleep for too long."

(For sometimes Snapperclogs goes to sleep for days and even weeks. Legend records that once, when he was lost and lonely, he went to sleep for a decade).

Suddenly, a gigantic
    snort and a yawn as
big as a boogle
    suggested that
    Snapperclogs had
    woken up.

"On we go"
    he glumped, and Fu
    clung to his
    redundant little wings
    while Archio jerked
    and fluttered about
    his head, trying to
    balance upon a
    flopping ear.

The three friends
  approached the Great
  Hillock of Blue Boogles
  just above the Stiggle
  Village to hear music
  close by.

"Hearken!"
          awked Archio,
"It must be the Stiggles
  singing their Stiggle
  song."

"I hope so,"
          said Fu,
"It always makes me
  feel very happy - and
  look at all the
  beautiful blue boogles
  here today!" he alerted
Snapperclogs.

"Buflumph!"
snuffled Snapperclogs.
I'm not ready for
another feast yet!"

As they came around
the hillock to the
Stiggle Village they
saw Gossip, Mao and
Beetle each sitting on
a little boogle stump
singing to all the
other stiggles who were
taking their afternoon
break.

"Hush,"
said Fu.
"Let us listen to their
song before we surprise
them."

They settled down just far enough behind the hillock so they could not be seen, Archio preening her feathers which had by now become quite dishevelled, whilst Fu nibbled at a length of stray pampas and Snapperclogs began to nod his head heavily as he found it more and more difficult to keep awake.

And they listened
attentively to the
Stiggles' gleeful
performance.

The Stiggles' Song

We're all friends and we share our troubles till we don't have troubles any more. A little bit of cheer, chortles and cuddles, thats what friends are for. If a Stiggle has a trouble he can chortle to his friend till he does'nt have a trouble any more lonely or sad, feeling bad, that's against the law! A very heavy log is half as heavy when two Stiggles can carry it

together. So the moral of our song is give and take then two Stiggles can be friends for ever. We're

very happy Stiggles 'cos we share our troubles till we don't have troubles any more. A

little bit of cheer chortles and cuddles thats what friends are

for. Yeah !

"Raah! Waaark! Bravi!"
cheered Fu and Archio
when the singing had
stopped and they
hurried around from
behind the hillock - so
startling Gossip, Mao
and Beetle that they
almost toppled off
their boogle stumps.

(A very unwise thing
to do).

But Snapperclogs had
fallen fast asleep
again, so, allowing
him his sleep this
time, Fu and Archio
chortled and chirped
to Gossip, Mao and

Beetle for a little while
before Archio shuffled
herself and yaaked

"Let us go and find
Lump, Fu, so we can
collect some grazzle
for my nest and
return to the woodland
before darkness."

Gossip told them where
Lump could be found
and off they went,
leaving Snapperclogs to
his beauty sleep, his
tummy rumbling and
the Stiggle hills
quaking as occasional
smokey belches emitted
from his twitching
nostrils.

Now Lump, who can easily be mistaken for a Stiggle hill, is quite unlike any other inhabitant of Evol. Indeed, he has no idea how he arrived there, nor does anyone else.

All we do know, as legend records, is that once upon a time, Lump had arrived in the Land lost and discontented with his previous existence, and he was looking for a safe and happy place to live his life.

But there was something very difficult about this. Lump found himself attracted to the Stiggle Village because something most peculiar inside him made him feel as though he wanted to eat Stiggles. This, of course, is quite unacceptable in the Land of Evol, so, if Lump was to live happily and contentedly, he would have to come to an agreement with the Stiggles.

Indeed, Lump had made
a pact with the
Stiggles the very day
he arrived in the
Stiggle Village. The
Stiggles would let him
live there forever more
if he promised that he
would never eat any
of them. It was
agreed that, in return
for this favour, all the
Stiggles would go to
the Stiggle Forest very
early each morning to
collect bracken and
fungus for Lump to
eat, and enough to
last him the whole
day through.

Legend tells that Lump
   had asked
"But what will I do with
   my life?"

Bo, the ancient leader of
   the Stiggles had
      pronounced

"Trumble, chortle on
   boogle stumps, make
   music, dream about
   good things at
   darkness and work
   for the Land, just as
   we all do in the Land
   of Evol."

All this sounded fair enough to Lump except for the fact that he was unable to perch on a boogle stump because of his quite unusual shape.

So, one day, all the Stiggles had gathered around him and had taught him how to rest his paws and snout upon one boogle stump and his back feet upon another very close by. This way he would be able to feel like a true part of the community.

Indeed Lump's contribution has always been most worthwhile.

For he reaps the grazzle and pushes away the noblets from the paths around the Stiggle Village to make it easier for the Stiggles to work. But he eats neither the grazzle nor the noblets for fear of offending the Stiggles. (Sometimes he is very hungry by the time the Stiggles return with his supper). Rather, he collects up the grazzle and stores it in a large heap for Archio so that she can build her nests.

Fu and Archio found
    Lump perched on two
boogle stumps with
many Stiggles dancing
all over him.   They
had just returned
from the Stiggle Forest
with his supper and
Lump was singing his
song to them to say
thank you.

Lump's Song

I don't know where I come from, I don't know why I'm here. I look

something like a boogle but I don't have have any fear 'cos they taught me how to chortle, they taught me how to cheer. In the

Land of Evol my freiends are always near.

It does'nt

matter what you look like, does'nt matter who you are.   In the   Land   of   Evol   everyone's   a   star

GUMP

"Hallo Lump!" said Fu.

"Aaahk!" squarked Archio.

"Humf!" said Lump.

The Stiggles all retired
to their Stiggle hills
to eat their own
suppers whilst Lump,
Fu and Archio chortled
about bamble boots,
fungus and Fig.   And
at the same time
Archio pecked the
dried mud from
Lump's coat to make
him feel good and to
say thank you for
collecting the grazzle
for her nest.

Then Fu and Archio were just about to pick up the day's harvest so that they could return to the woodland before darkness, when the land resounded with a long, loud shrill coming from the Great Hillock of Blue Boogles above the Stiggle Village.

It was Toe-Toe, Fig's messenger, sounding the Great Golden Horn of Evol.

Everyone round about stood absolutely still and quiet.

'It must be a very important announcement,' they thought, for the Great Golden Horn of Evol is only ever sounded at the most important of occasions.

All the Stiggles scuttled out of their homes quickly towards the foot of the hillock.

Fu trumbled with Archio fluttering alongside.

Lump lolloped as fast as he was able.

Glibalobs could be seen trumbling at speed up the hillock towards Toe-Toe.

(For Glibalobs is always
the first to collect a
message from Toe-Toe
whose voice is so
small that he can
only ever whisper a
tiny breath).

Gramblesnip followed
closely behind Glibalobs
and Toe-Toe chortled
for one brief moment.
Then Toe-Toe stepped
into a cloud and
disappeared as
Glibalobs turned and
perched upon a boogle
stump.

He put his head in his hands and a tear ran to the tip of his nose.

Gramblesnip perched beside Glibalobs who uttered a word or two into his little ear.

Without delay Gramblesnip trumbled down the hillock to pass on the news to all the inhabitants of Evol.

"What could it be?"'
"What is the news?"

came chortles and whispers from all around.

Gramblesnip mumbled the news to Fu who relayed it to Gossip, Mao and Beetle, and so to all the eagerly waiting Stiggles, and Lump was the last to be informed.

The atmosphere was tense and the whispers and chortling became louder and louder until the sad, oh sad news was echoing all over the Stiggle Village and indeed all around the entire Land of Evol.

"Snapperclogs has gone to sleep forever"
the sad voices told.

Then the chortling
quietened and there
was silence and
stillness as all the
inhabitants of the
Land looked towards
the Old Oak Tree of
Evol.

A great light was
shining down on the
place where
Snapperclogs had been
resting on the other
side of the hillock.

Each and every creature
of Evol perched upon
one of the many boogle
stumps around the
hillock.

They put their heads
together and shared
their tears.

"What are we going to
do without
Snapperclogs?" they
sobbed.   "How will we
ever be happy again?"

Then, with loud and resounding music all around, the shaft of light lifted from Snapperclogs' resting place and broadened into the centre of the sky, brighter than had ever been seen before. Not even the Great Golden Fire had ever given such a light, a warmth or a brilliance.

All the inhabitants of Evol rose from the boogle stumps, looked up to the wonderful light and Fig appeared, in all his splendour, glorious and colourful, with a broad and happy smile and creases around his eyes.

He looked over all of
the Land and spoke in
a great, commanding
voice.

"My dear friends of
Evol, now that
Snapperclogs has gone
to rest forever, I must
tell you the secret of
the Land of Evol.

The secret of the Land
of Evol . . . is . . . .
the boogle stump.
The boogle stump is
alive."

The Clobs, Stiggles and
other creatures all
gasped with surprise.

"But the boogle stump is only alive when it has turned to stone, after its' head has been eaten off by Snapperclogs.

And, when perched upon, the boogle stump sends patters of wisdom and love into the earth where I cannot reach.

I can only reach you, but *you* can reach the boogle stump."

"Therefore, it is up to you, not me, to put love into the Land, for it is your land, not mine.

I can only give you a little guidance, when you allow me to do so, but I can assure you that love is eternal if you believe in it and if you work for it.

You must love the boogle stump as you love one another, always perch upon it weasily, and you must always respect and honour the Old Oak Tree of Evol."

"Now that Snapperclogs is no longer with us, you must go out all over the land and work hard at taking off the boogle tops yourselves, perch on as many boogle stumps as you can find and as often as you find them.

Work hard at your loving and, **one** day, Snapperclogs may return to the Land of Evol."

Fig's voice was filled with hope and comforting as he continued.

"Dear friends, let me tell you, all things grow from the Land, so the love you put into it through the boogle stump is all important for Evol. Indeed, it is this very thing which makes the Land of Evol **Evolve.**

Yes, it is how we grow through generation to generation, learning and becoming greater and wiser all the while.

My dear friends, this is the secret of **Evolution**."

"Everyone is welcome in the Land of Evol. Yes, even you who are reading this story. But remember . . . there is no evil in the Land of Evol, no greed and no fighting. Only friendship, sharing and love.

And remember too . . .
the boogle stump is
always asleep, and if
the boogle stump is
woken up it turns
back into a headless
mushroom, withers and
dies.

And **this** is why you
have to perch on a
boogle stump weasily."

Fig faded back into the distant skies far beyond the Great Golden Fire, and all the inhabitants of Evol trumbled off around the land, chortling and singing solemnly to one another.

They worked hard at turning boogles into boogle stumps.

They worked hard at their friendships, sharing and loving, and Evol remained the happiest land in the Universe.

The End